Lucy Ladybird didn't belong anywhere.

"You can't be one of us," cried the other ladybirds.

"You have no spots!"

Lucy flew off, feeling sad and alone. The hot summer sun glared uncomfortably down on her.

Suddenly, she noticed Fred Frog.

"Fred Frog!" said Lucy. "You are so beautiful with your smooth GREEN spots. I wish I could be like you."

"But Lucy Ladybird," croaked Fred Frog, "YOU are beautiful too. You float so smoothly through the air!"

"If you really want spots, please have one of mine. I have plenty to spare."

Lucy was so happy. Now she had ONE spot!

Before long, autumn arrived and the leaves turned orange, red and yellow, then floated gently to the ground. Lucy was admiring them as Carla Caterpillar cycled by.

"Carla Caterpillar!" cried Lucy. "You are so beautiful with your shiny YELLOW spots. I wish I could be like you."

"But Lucy Ladybird," said Carla Caterpillar, "YOU are so beautiful with your shiny red wings. You can fly so fast!"

."I have lots and lots of spots. Please take one of mine."

Lucy was so happy. Now she had TWO spots!

The land grew cold with frost and icicles as winter approached. Lucy was watching the pretty snowflakes dance in the air, turning everything white, when Felicity Fish jumped up from the pond.

"Felicity Fish!" called Lucy. "You are so beautiful with your sparkling BLUE spots. I wish I could be like you."

"But Lucy Ladybird," said Felicity Fish, "YOU are beautiful too! You have such lovely sparkling eyes!"

"If spots are what you want, please have one of mine."

Lucy was so happy. Now she had THREE spots!

It wasn't long before spring arrived and the flowers awoke from their long slumber. Lucy was enjoying their sweet scent when she saw Bella Bird.

"Bella Bird!" called Lucy. "You are so beautiful with your dazzling WHITE spots. I wish I could be like you."

"But Lucy Ladybird," cried Bella, "YOU are beautiful too. You make everyone so happy with your dazzling smile!"

"If you'd like an extra spot, please take one of mine."

Lucy was so happy. Now she had FOUR spots!

For the very first time, Lucy felt
like a real ladybird! She smiled at
the thought of her four spots as she
made her way back home...

... past dazzling
Bella Bird...

... past sparkling
Felicity Fish...

... past Carla Caterpillar,
now transformed into
a beautiful, shiny butterfly...

... and over smooth-spotted
Fred Frog, jumping
cheerfully through the air.

Lucy returned from her journey with her four
beautiful spots: one smooth green spot,
one shiny yellow spot,
one sparkling blue spot,
and one dazzling white spot.

She suddenly realised that she still
didn't fit in with the other ladybirds.

All their spots were black!